Y0-CJF-201

SEP 0 8 2006

J 743 .89 COU
Court, Rob, 1956-
How to draw action sports
figures /

PALM BEACH COUNTY
LIBRARY SYSTEM
3650 SUMMIT BLVD.
WEST PALM BEACH, FLORIDA 33406

How to Draw
Action Sports Figures

This book is dedicated to Jesse Dean.

The Child's World

Published in the United States of America by The Child's World®
PO Box 326 • Chanhassen, MN 55317-0326
800-599-READ • www.childsworld.com

Acknowledgments
Design and Production: The Creative Spark, San Juan Capistrano, CA
Series Editor: Elizabeth Sirimarco Budd
Illustration: Rob Court

Registration
The Child's World® and associated logo is the sole property and registered trademark of The Child's World®.
The Scribbles Institute™, Young Artist Basics, and their associated logos are the sole property and registered trademarks of The Scribbles Institute™. Copyright © 2005 The Scribbles Institute™. All rights reserved. No part of this book may be reproduced or utilized in any form or by any means without permission from the publisher.

Library of Congress Cataloging-in-Publication Data
Court, Rob, 1956–
  How to draw action sports figures / by Rob Court.
      p. cm. — (The Scribbles Institute)
  ISBN 1-59296-147-9 (library bound : alk. paper)
 1. Sports in art—Juvenile literature. 2. Athletes in art—Juvenile literature. 3. Drawing—Technique—Juvenile literature. I. Title.
  NC825.S62C68 2004
  743'.89796—dc22
                                                    2004003728

The Scribbles Institute™ How-to-Draw Books

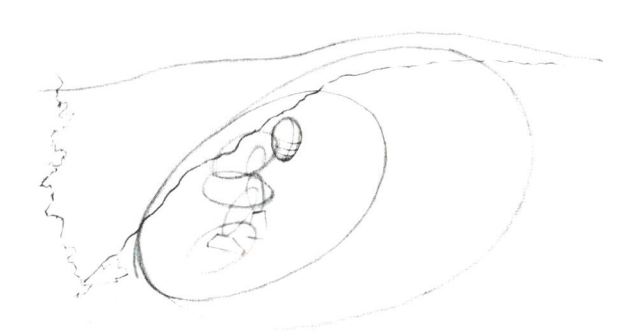

How to Draw
Action Sports Figures

Rob Court

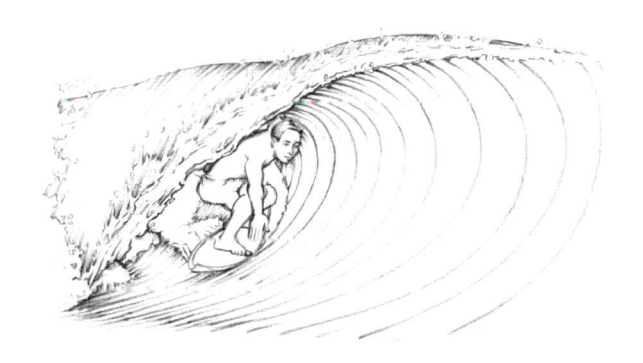

The Child's World®

*It is not enough to believe what you see,
you must also understand what you see.*

—Leonardo da Vinci

Parents and Teachers,

Children love to draw! It is an essential part of a child's learning process. Drawing skills are used to investigate both natural and constructed environments, record observations, solve problems, and express ideas. The purpose of this book is to help students advance through the challenges of drawing and to encourage the use of drawing in school projects. The reader is also introduced to the elements of visual art—lines, shapes, patterns, form, texture, light, space, and color—and their importance in the fundamentals of drawing.

The Scribbles Institute is devoted to educational materials that keep creativity in our schools and in our children's dreams. Our mission is to empower young creative thinkers with knowledge in visual art while helping to improve their drawing skills. Students, parents, and teachers are invited to visit our Web site—www.scribblesinstitute.com—for useful information and guidance. You can even get advice from a drawing coach!

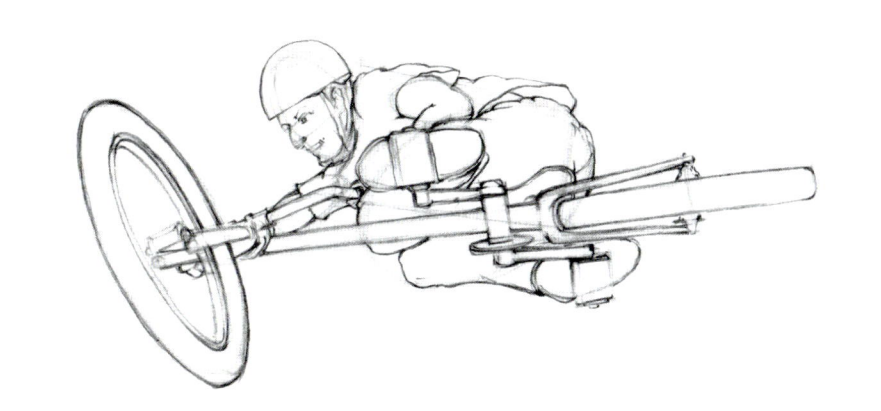

Contents

Drawing Action Sports Figures	6
Drawing with Shapes	8
Drawing with Lines	9
Drawing the Head	10
Three-Dimensional Form	16
Light and Shadows	18
Patterns	20
Texture	22
Space and Composition	24
Drawing with Color	28
The Artist's Studio	31
Glossary	32
Index	32

Drawing Action Sports Figures

It's exciting to draw a skateboarder performing a kick-flip. Or to draw surfers, snowboarders, and BMX riders as they perform difficult tricks. Learning to draw the human figure in action poses can help improve your drawing skills.

The easy steps in this book will help you draw action sports figures. Find a big piece of paper and a pencil. You can get started right now!

Proportions

The height of an adult human figure is about eight heads tall. The body of a surfer, shown at right, is divided into sections by head height. This shows the **proportions** of his body. Knowing the proportions of a figure helps to make your drawing realistic.

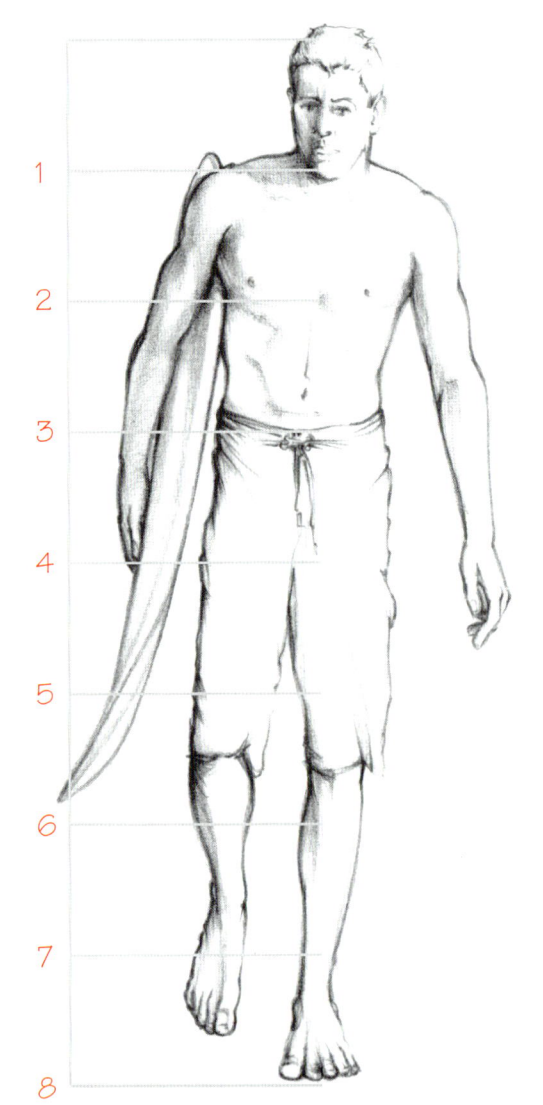

Look for Shapes and Hidden Curves

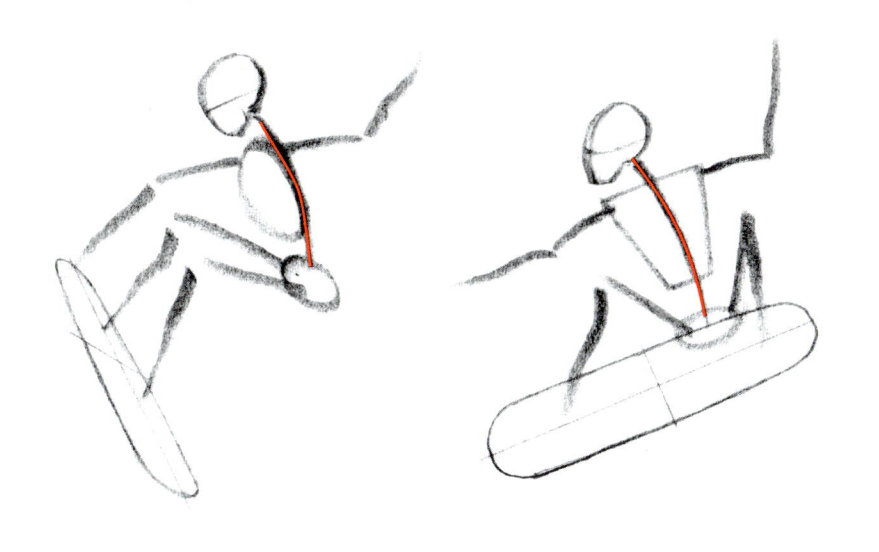

Start by sketching the basic shapes of your figure. This helps to position the head, body, and sports equipment before drawing the final details. Look for the curves that connect the shapes of the body and show its position in action.

Center of Gravity and Zero Gravity

On the next page, you'll learn to draw a snowboarder. The point where her body weight is centered is called the center of gravity. To keep her balance in extreme situations, she keeps her center of gravity low, over the top of the snowboard. At the highest point of a turn, her body becomes weightless, like an astronaut in outer space. This moment is called zero gravity, and it's exciting to draw.

center of gravity

Drawing with Shapes

Drawing an action sports figure is easy when you start with basic shapes. Oval shapes show the position of her head and body. Sketch these shapes lightly. This way, you can erase them later as you finish your picture.

Snowboarder

1 You're seeing this snowboarder in the air, grabbing the edge of her snowboard. She's at the highest point of her turn (zero gravity). Her knees almost touch her chest. Start by sketching oval shapes for her head and body. Now draw the shape that shows the position of her snowboard.

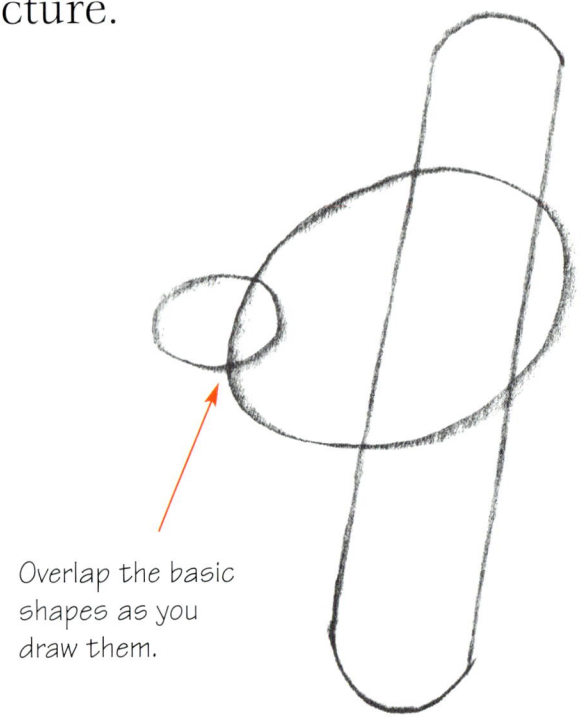

Overlap the basic shapes as you draw them.

2 Sketch ovals for the parts of her arms that you can see. Next, draw the shapes for her hands and knees. Add the rectangular shape for her goggles and the shapes of her nose and mouth. See page 10 for help drawing the front view of a face.

HOT TIP

Foreshortening

You can't see the entire length of the boarder's legs and right arm. The legs and arm look as if they are coming toward you. So you must draw their shortened form. This is called foreshortening.

Drawing with Lines

Now draw an **outline** around the edge of the shapes you've made. This will be her body and her snowboard. Keep drawing until you like the outline. Remember to draw lightly so that you can erase if necessary.

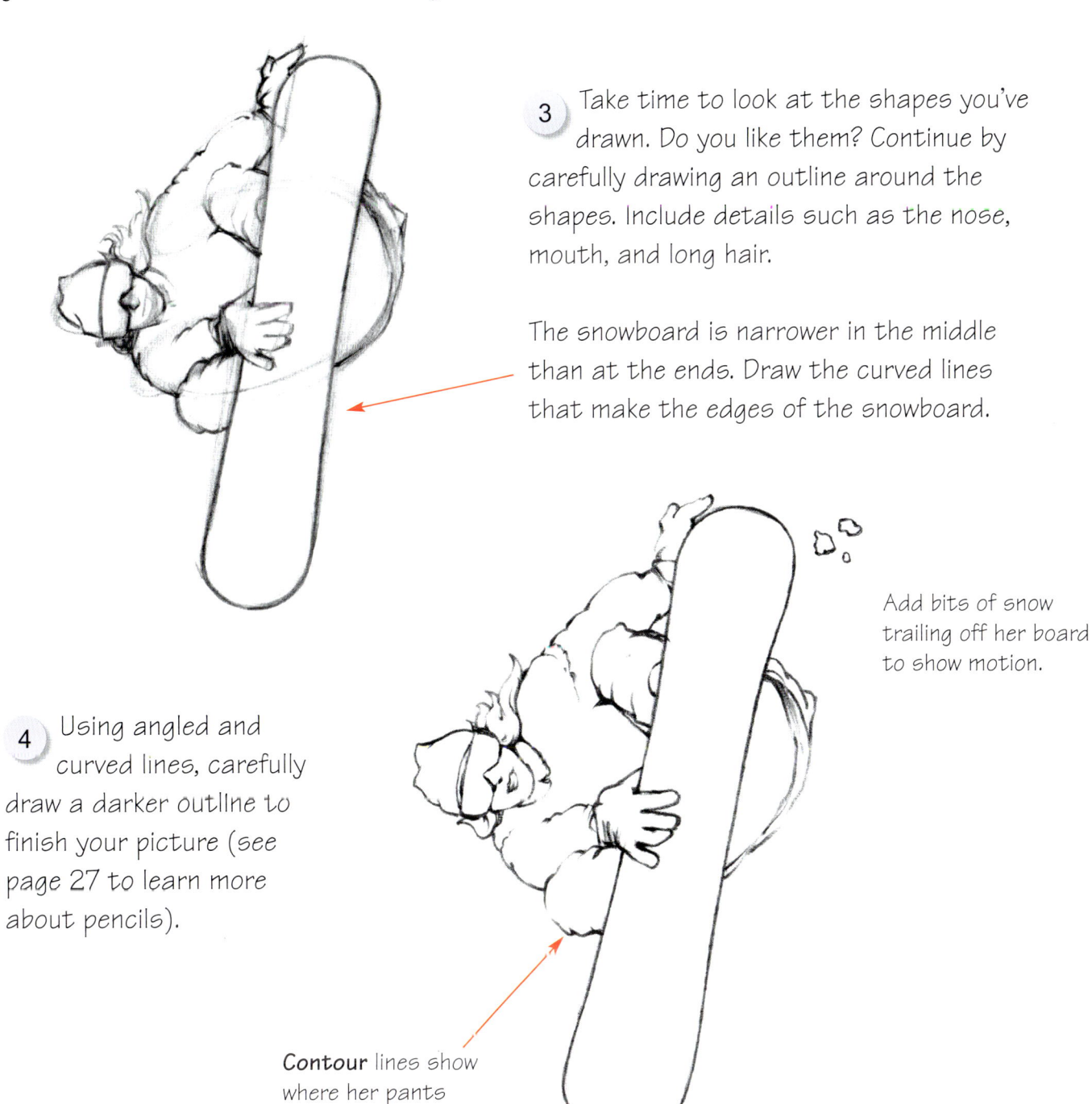

3. Take time to look at the shapes you've drawn. Do you like them? Continue by carefully drawing an outline around the shapes. Include details such as the nose, mouth, and long hair.

The snowboard is narrower in the middle than at the ends. Draw the curved lines that make the edges of the snowboard.

Add bits of snow trailing off her board to show motion.

4. Using angled and curved lines, carefully draw a darker outline to finish your picture (see page 27 to learn more about pencils).

Contour lines show where her pants fold at the knees.

Drawing the Head

By using shapes and lines, you can draw a head that looks realistic. With practice, you'll be able to draw different views of the head with correct proportions.

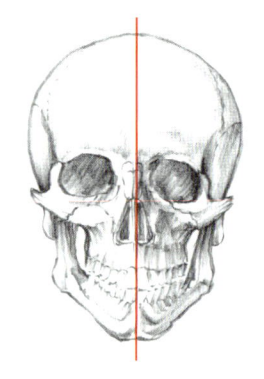

Front View

The shape of the head is based on the shape of the skull. When looking at the skull from the front, an imaginary line divides it in half.

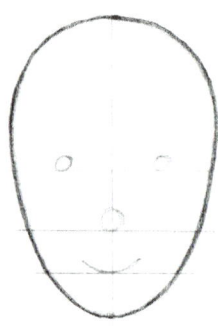

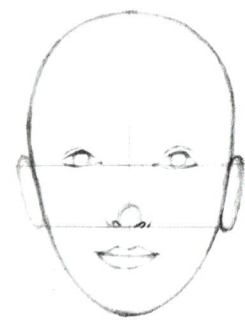

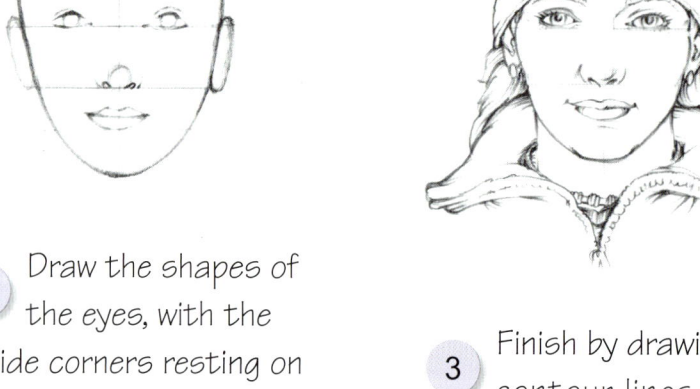

1. Sketch an egg shape for the head. Divide it equally by drawing **horizontal** and **vertical** guidelines. Next, draw two small circles for eyeballs and a circle for the nose. A curved line shows the bottom lip.

2. Draw the shapes of the eyes, with the inside corners resting on the horizontal line. Then sketch the outlines for the upper and lower lips. Place ovals for the ears between the top of the eyes and the bottom of the nose.

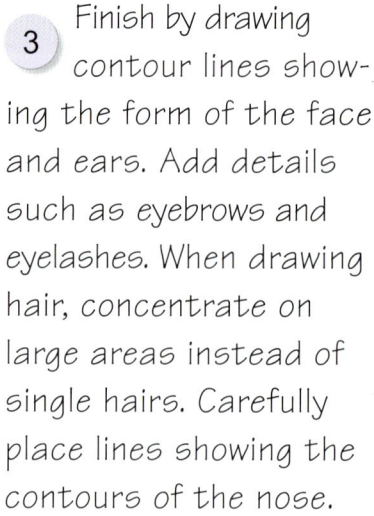

3. Finish by drawing contour lines showing the form of the face and ears. Add details such as eyebrows and eyelashes. When drawing hair, concentrate on large areas instead of single hairs. Carefully place lines showing the contours of the nose.

HOT TIP
The width of the head is five eyes across.

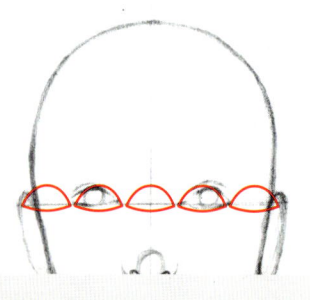

10

Profile

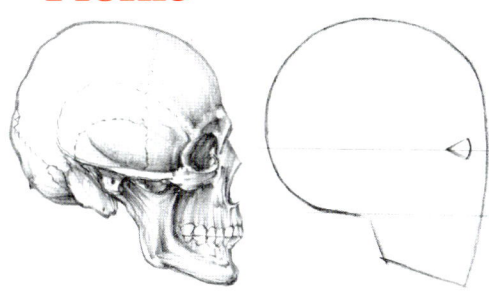

1 A profile, or side view, of the skull shows the proportions of the head. Start by drawing the shape for the head. Divide it equally, as shown above. Draw lines for the area of the face and jaw. Add the shape for the eye.

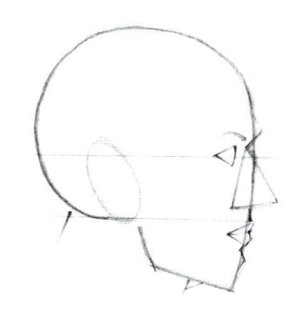

2 Use the guidelines to position an oval for the ear. Sketch outlines for the nose, mouth, and chin.

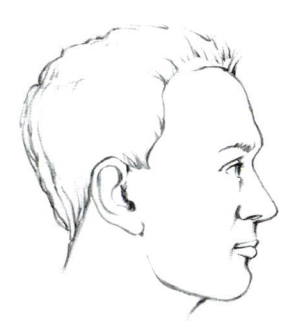

3 Finish the profile by drawing contour lines around the forehead, nose, mouth, chin, and neck. Draw lines that show the hair, the eyebrow, and the corner of the mouth.

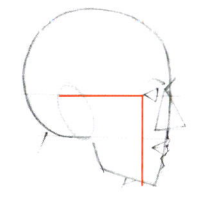

HOT TIP

The distance from the corner of the eye to the back of the ear is the same as the distance from the corner of the eye to the chin.

Three-Quarter View

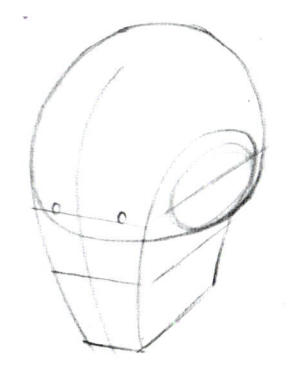

1 Between the front view and profile is the three-quarter view. The proportions are the same as the front and profile, but the guidelines wrap around the form of the head. Start by dividing an egg shape as shown above.

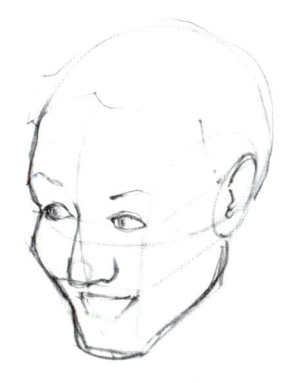

2 Use the guidelines to position an oval for the ear. Now sketch outlines for the nose, mouth, and chin.

3 Finish the three-quarter view by drawing contour lines around the forehead, nose, mouth, and chin. Notice how you see less of the right side of the mouth and cheek. Add details such as hair and eyebrows.

You can draw many kinds of action sports figures. By starting with basic shapes, you can show the position of a BMX rider's head and body, as well as his bike.

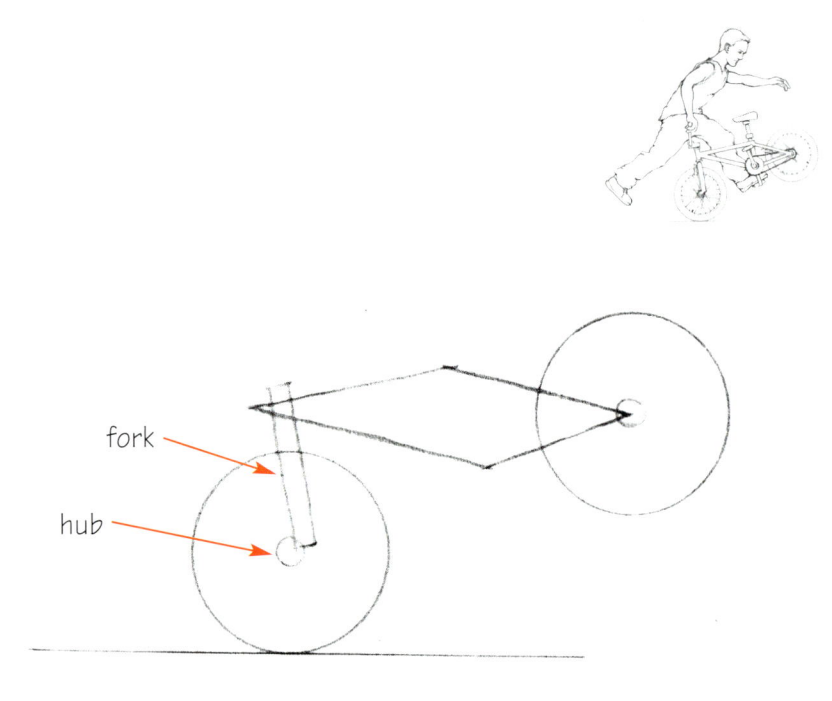

BMX Rider

fork

hub

1 Begin by drawing a horizontal line for the ground. Then sketch two circles for the wheels. Notice the rear wheel is higher above ground than the front wheel. Sketch two small circles for the hubs at the center of each wheel. Draw a long, narrow rectangle that will be the fork. Now draw a long diamond shape for the bike's frame.

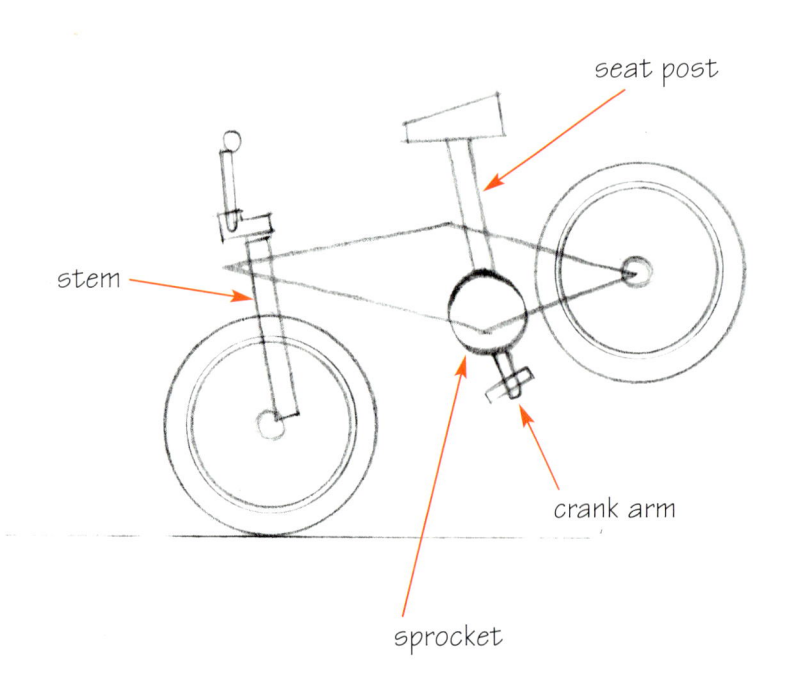

seat post

stem

crank arm

sprocket

2 Sketch a smaller circle for the sprocket. Carefully add the rectangles that make the crank arms and pedals. Now sketch a long, narrow rectangle for the seat post. Its angle should match the fork. Draw the shape for the seat. Next, draw the rectangles that show the position of the handlebars. Add circles for the handle's grip and wheel rims.

Drawing Circles

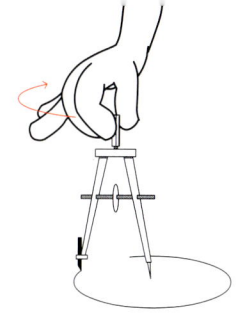

HOT TIP

When drawing circles, practice moving your whole hand. You can also use a circle guide or compass to make circles.

3. It's time to draw the shapes that show the position of the rider's body. Start by sketching the angled shape for his pants. Next, draw the shapes of his shoes. Notice how his shoe is positioned on the pedal. Now sketch an oval for his upper body and an egg shape for his head. A line makes the neck bones that connect his head and body.

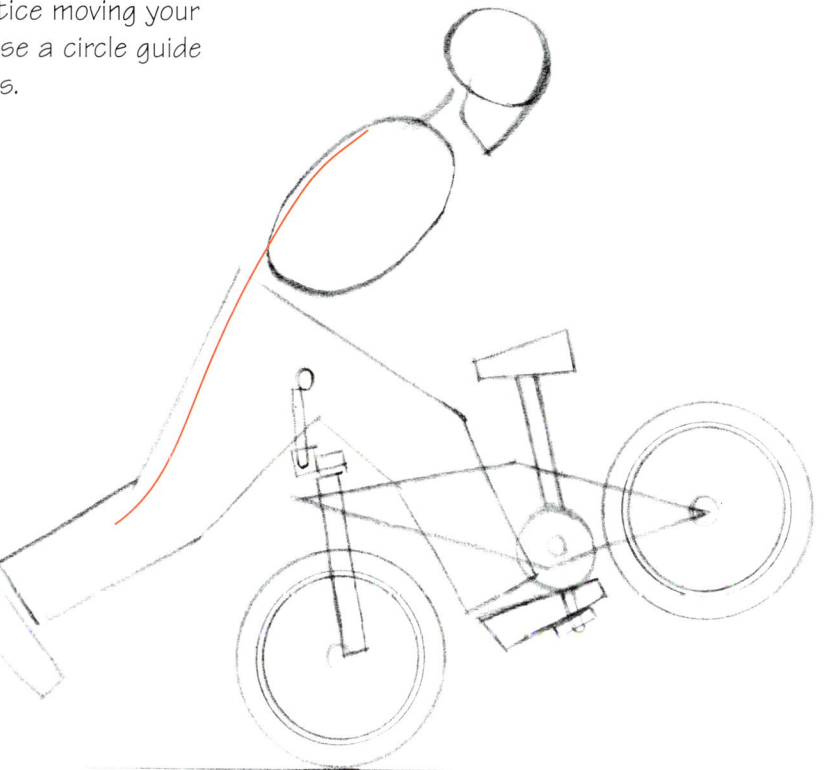

Imagine the rider's weight balanced over the front wheel. Look for the hidden curve in his back and leg.

4. Lightly sketch the ovals for his arms. Now add the shapes for his hands. Notice how his right hand fits around the circle of the handle grip.

13

Draw outlines around the edges of the shapes you've made. This will be the BMX rider's bike and his body. Keep drawing until you like the outline. Remember to draw lightly.

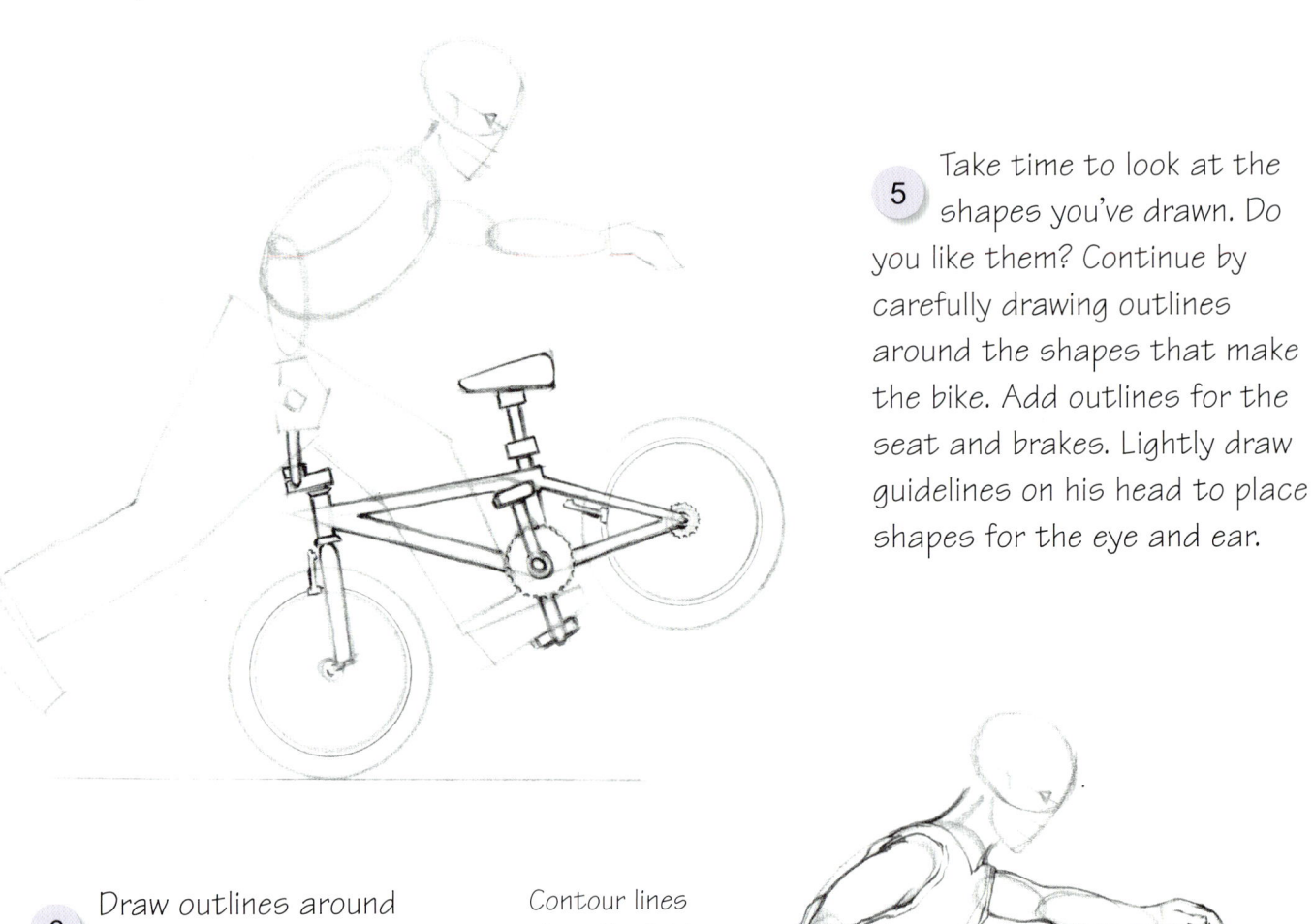

5 Take time to look at the shapes you've drawn. Do you like them? Continue by carefully drawing outlines around the shapes that make the bike. Add outlines for the seat and brakes. Lightly draw guidelines on his head to place shapes for the eye and ear.

6 Draw outlines around the edges of the rider's pants. Keep sketching until you like the contours you've drawn. Draw the contours of his shirt and shoes. His clothing will look more realistic if you show areas that stretch or fold. Sketch outlines that form his arms and hands.

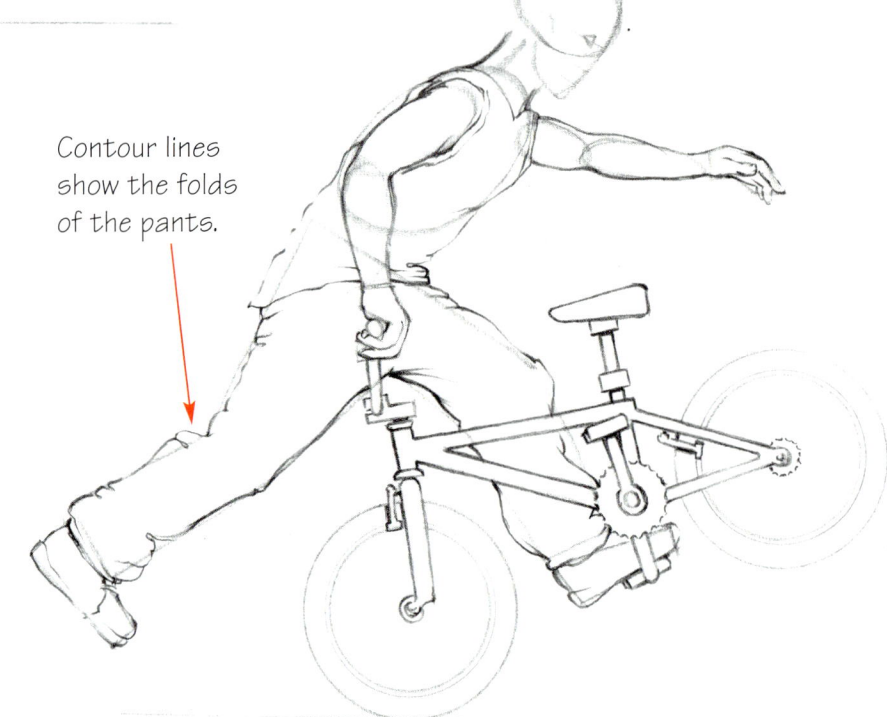

Contour lines show the folds of the pants.

7 Look at the outlines you've made for the rider's body and bike. Do you like the form of his arms and hands? Make corrections by lightly redrawing the contour lines. Sketch details such as his hair, eyes, nose, mouth, and fingers. There are many details in this drawing. Take time to include as many as you can.

Use curved lines, not straight lines, to draw the rider's back.

8 Using angled and curved lines, draw darker outlines to finish your picture. Notice the flowing, curved lines of his body compared with the straighter, angled lines of his bike frame. How is the line used for the chain different from the other lines?

The wheels aren't spinning, so you can see the spokes. Draw a pattern of straight lines for the spokes.

15

Three-Dimensional Form

It's time to make people and things look real. With practice, you can change flat shapes into three-dimensional or "3-D" form. By repeating curved lines, you can illustrate the form of a wave breaking over a surfer.

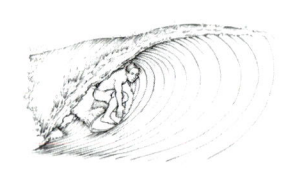

Surfer

1 Sketch an oval for the area of the wave that is closest to the surfer's body. Next, make a larger oval for the overall form of the wave. Now draw the ovals that make his legs and upper body. Place an egg shape for his head. A curved line makes the top edge of the wave.

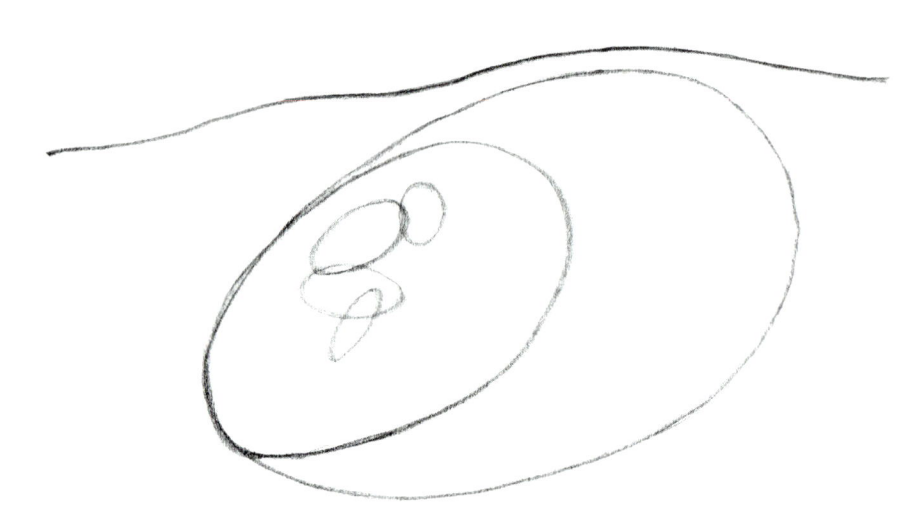

These shapes show the surfer's low center of gravity and his position in the wave.

2 Sketch ovals for his arms and the shapes that make his hands and feet. Next, sketch the shape for the surfboard. Draw the guidelines for his face. Now draw the line that shows the part of the wave moving over his head and crashing down to the left of his body.

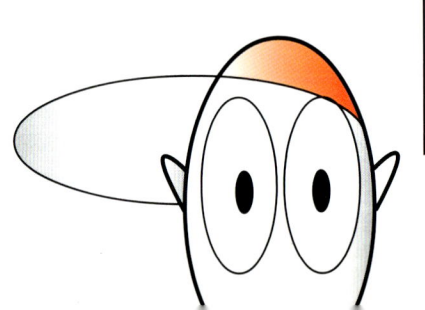

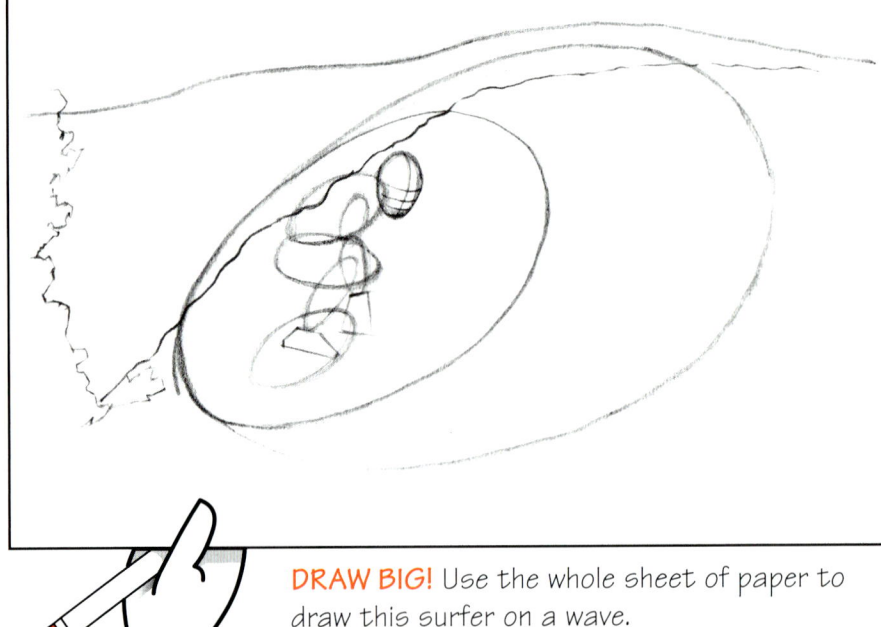

DRAW BIG! Use the whole sheet of paper to draw this surfer on a wave.

3 Begin drawing the outlines around the shapes that form the surfer's body. Take time to draw the contours of his arm and leg muscles. Draw his eyes, nose, and mouth using guidelines for positioning. To show the 3-D form of the wave, continue drawing lines that follow the curves of the oval and egg shapes you've made for the wave.

Add details of the whitewater part of the wave as it moves over the surfer's head. Smaller water drops show the motion of the wave.

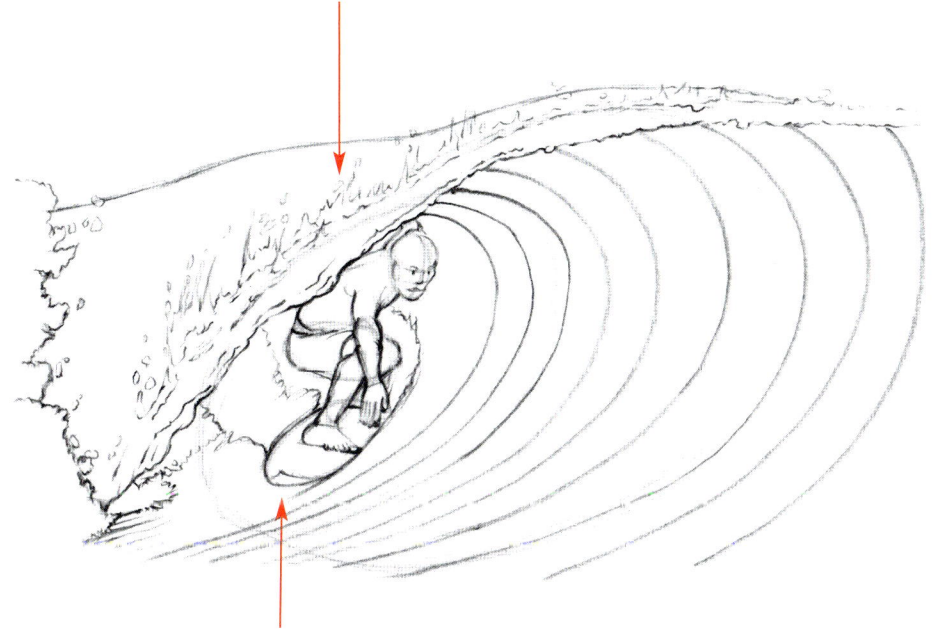

Add lines that form the surfboard's turned-up nose.

4 Continue repeating curved lines that form the face of the wave. Draw darker outlines of details such as the spray of the wave. Finish by drawing the darker contour lines of the surfer's body, his surfboard, and the wave. His eyes should be looking in the direction he is traveling.

Shorter, curved lines show darker areas of the wave.

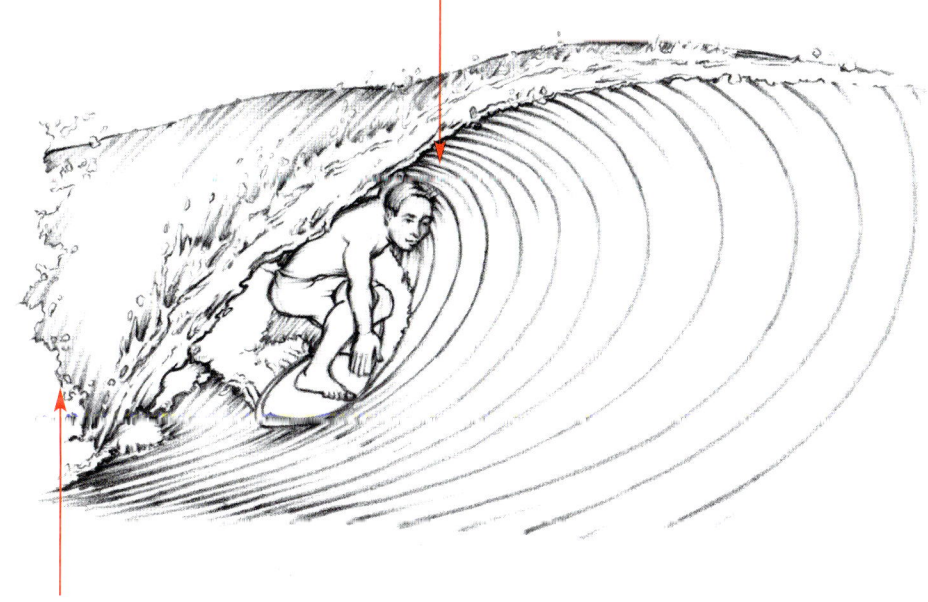

Add lines to show the wave behind the whitewater.

17

Light and Shadows

Tones are lighter and darker shades of a color. By using tones, you can create shadows. This helps you see the form of a skateboarder and the roundness of a cylinder-shaped trash barrel.

Skateboarder

1. Start with basic shapes to draw this skater doing a kick-flip over a barrel. Sketch the shapes that make his head and body. Next, carefully position the shape of his skateboard above a narrow oval that makes the top of the barrel.

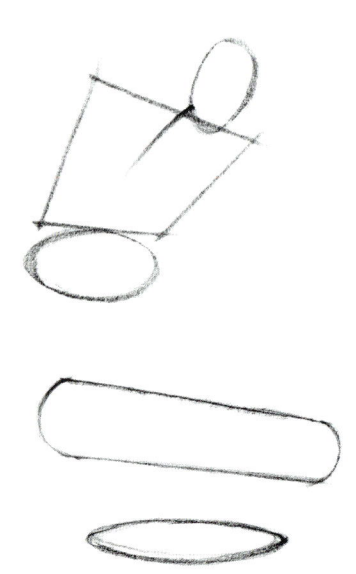

Guidelines

Press lightly with your pencil when drawing the guidelines that make these basic shapes. This makes it easier to erase the shapes before drawing the shadows shown in step 4.

2. His body and skateboard are floating above the top of the barrel, in zero gravity. Sketch the shapes for his legs, arms, and hands. Add guidelines for his head to place the lines for his eyes. Sketch the lines for his hat. Make two small ovals for the skateboard wheels. Next, draw an oval for the bottom of the barrel and the two straight lines for its sides.

Light Source

Places where light comes from are called light sources. The sun is a light source. A lamp is also a light source. In the drawing below, a light source shines on a sphere. How do the shadows change as the light changes position?

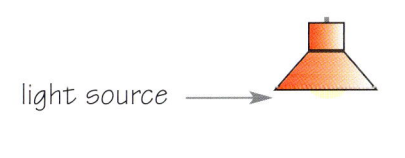

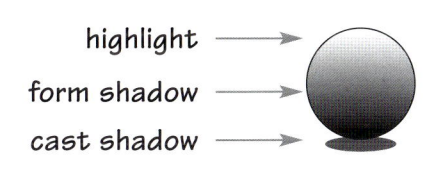

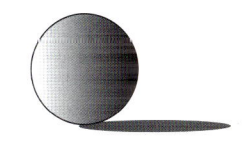

light source

highlight
form shadow
cast shadow

3 Before you add shadows, draw the outlines that form the body, skateboard, and barrel. Add details for the skateboarder's face and the contours of his clothes. Carefully erase all the guidelines before shading.

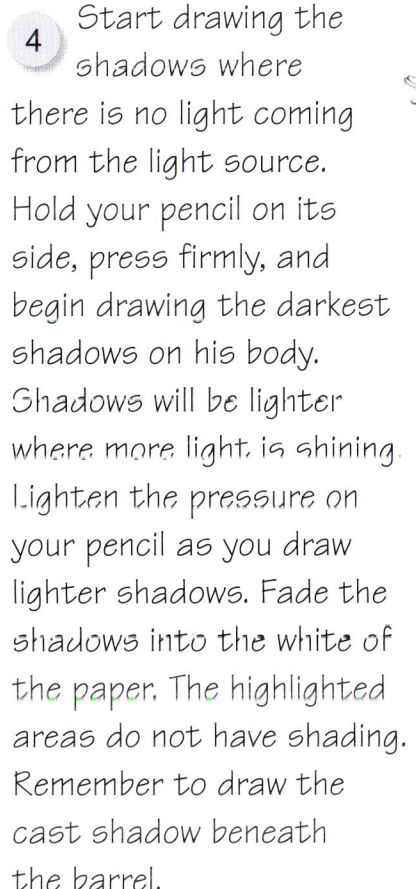

4 Start drawing the shadows where there is no light coming from the light source. Hold your pencil on its side, press firmly, and begin drawing the darkest shadows on his body. Shadows will be lighter where more light is shining. Lighten the pressure on your pencil as you draw lighter shadows. Fade the shadows into the white of the paper. The highlighted areas do not have shading. Remember to draw the cast shadow beneath the barrel.

Patterns

By repeating lines or shapes, you can draw patterns. Patterns make the picture of a BMX rider more interesting and realistic.

BMX Rider

1 The BMX rider is high in the air, performing an aerial. We are looking directly at the bottom of his bike. His knees are bent, almost touching his chest. Start by sketching an oval and rectangle shape for his body. Next, draw an egg shape for his head. Now draw a long, narrow rectangle shape for the position of his bike frame and rear tire. Add an oval for the front tire.

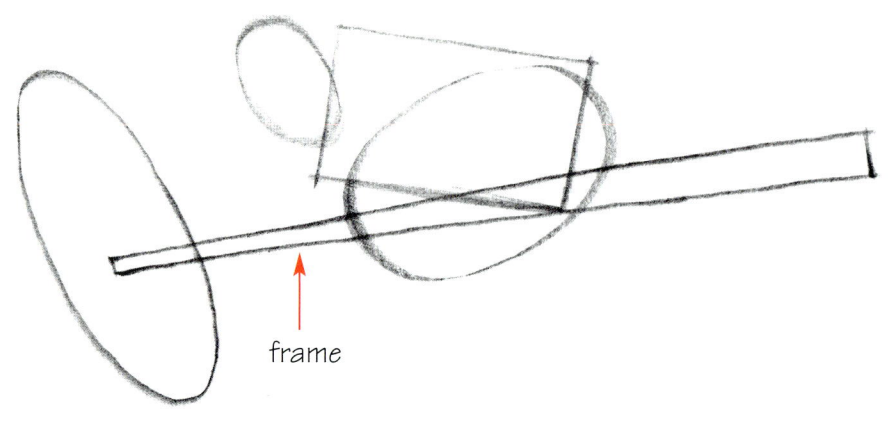

frame

2 Take time to draw the various shapes that form his bike. A rectangle makes the fork. Add another oval for the rim of his front tire. A small cylinder shape makes the hub of his front wheel. Straight lines make the frame and hub for the rear wheel. Add rectangles for the pedals. Now add ovals for his arms and the shapes for the bottom of his shoes. Sketch the guidelines for his face and the ovals for his eye and ear.

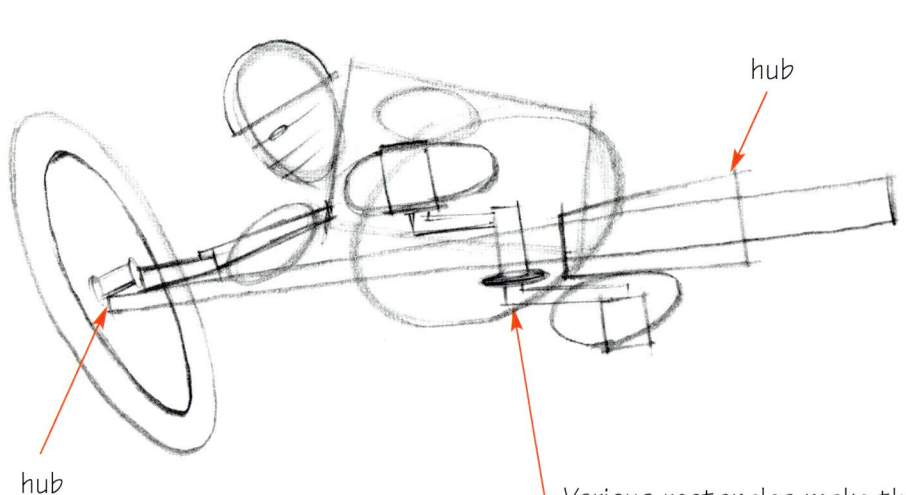

hub

hub

Various rectangles make the crank set at the bottom of the bike frame.

20

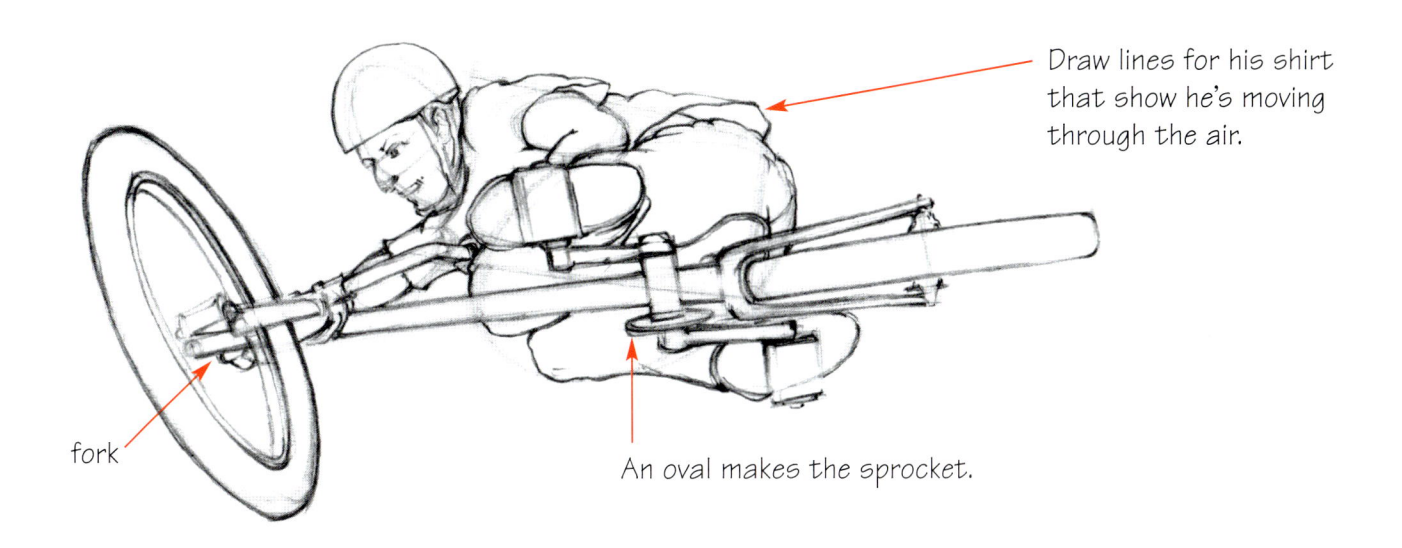

Draw lines for his shirt that show he's moving through the air.

fork

An oval makes the sprocket.

3 Do you like the position of the shapes you've drawn? Continue by carefully sketching the outlines that form his body and the parts of his bike. This is called tightening your drawing. Pay attention to the curved lines that form the edges of the front and rear tires. Draw the contours of his face and the folds of his clothing. His strong arms hold the handlebars steady.

4 Finish your drawing by carefully sketching a darker outline for the final contours of the BMX rider. Now it's time to add lines that make the patterns for the bottoms of his shoes. Repeat straight and angled lines that make the patterns for the treads of the tires. Take time to tighten the final outlines of the frame of his bike. Finish with details for his face, helmet and chain on the sprocket.

Action lines make the wheel look like it's spinning.

21

Texture

How the surface of something feels is called its texture. The texture of snow is different from the texture of rocks and trees. You can draw lines and patterns to create different textures.

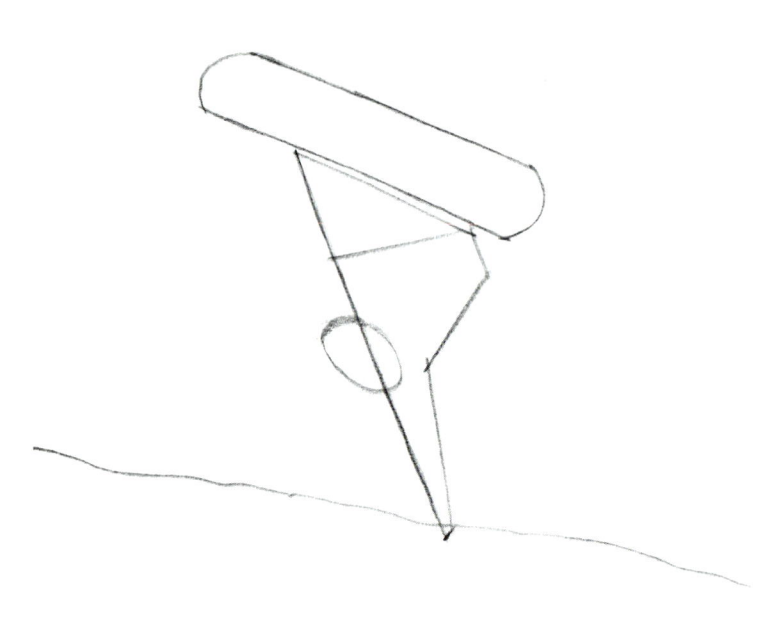

Snowboarder

1 This snowboarder is performing an invert at the top of a half-pipe. His body is balanced on his hand. Begin your drawing by sketching angled lines for the overall shape of his body. Draw an oval for his head. Next, make the basic shape of the snowboard. Lightly draw an angled line to show the top edge of the half-pipe.

2 Notice the compact position of his body. One knee almost touches his chest. His arm is extended, supporting his weight. Sketch ovals for the muscles of his arms and legs. Make the shapes for his gloves and goggles.

Begin sketching lines to create objects behind the snowboarder. The space behind him is called the background. Lightly sketch the position of rocks and trees. The snowboarder is in the foreground of the picture.

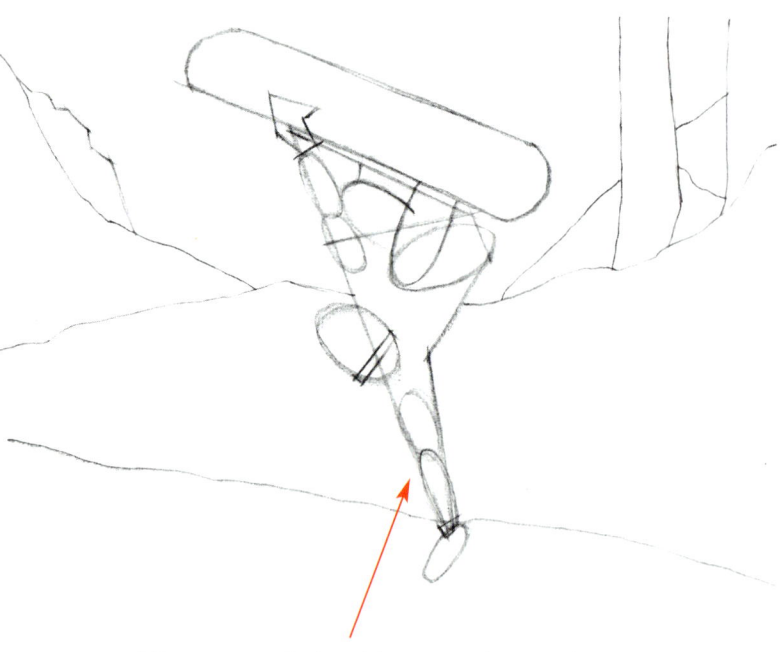

His arm and shoulder muscles work together to balance his weight.

His head faces down the wall where he will land.

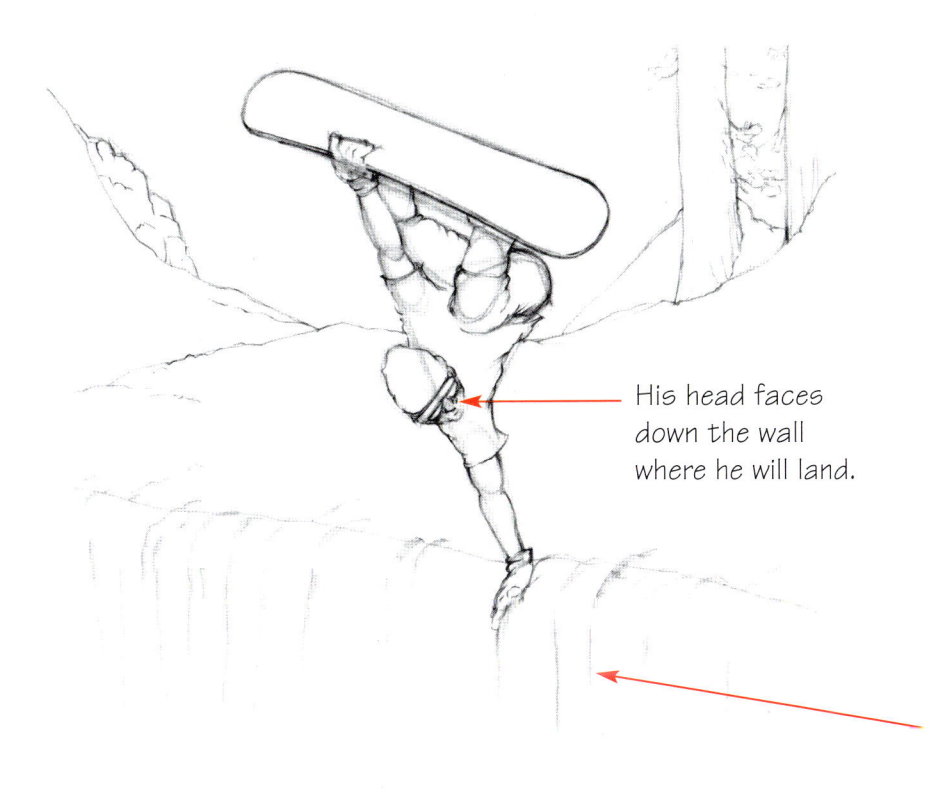

3 Begin drawing outlines for his body. Sketch the contour lines for his clothing and the edges of his board. Keep sketching outlines of his arm muscles and details of his head until you like their form.

Draw angled lines to show the texture of the rocks and trees in the background. Use softer lines to make the snow.

Straighter lines show the icy, vertical wall of the half-pipe.

4 Draw the texture of the trees by using broken, jagged lines. Add more lines to show details of the rocks and wall of the half-pipe. Next, look at the form of the snowboarder. If you like what you've drawn, then continue with darker contour lines to finish your drawing. A darker outline will make him look as if he is in front of the rocks and tree.

HOT TIP

This basic pose can also be used when drawing a skateboarder performing an invert.

23

Space and Composition

The white space on your paper can be transformed into an environment where a skateboarder rides on a cement cube. The way you divide the space is called composition. Begin your composition by drawing the horizon line. This shows where the ground meets the sky. Draw it to the edges of your paper. Now begin drawing the shape of the cube.

Skateboarder

1. To draw the cube, you can use a way of drawing called **perspective,** which makes things appear farther away in space. Start by drawing the horizon line. This shows where the sky meets the ground. Next, draw a dot at each end of the horizon line. Now draw a straight, vertical line. This is the corner of the cube that is nearest to you.

2. Lightly draw straight lines from the top of the vertical line to each vanishing point. Next, draw straight lines from the bottom of the vertical line to each vanishing point. You can use a ruler to draw these guidelines. To complete the cube, make vertical lines where you want to place the two corners in the distance.

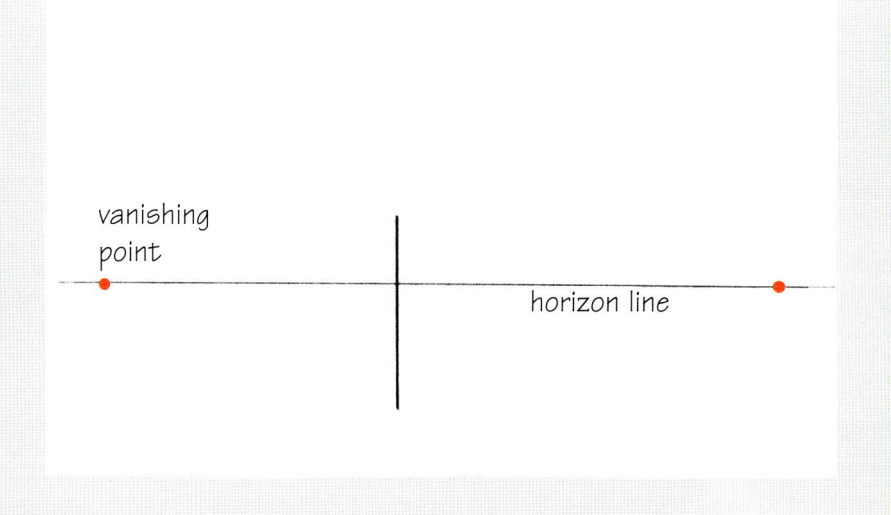

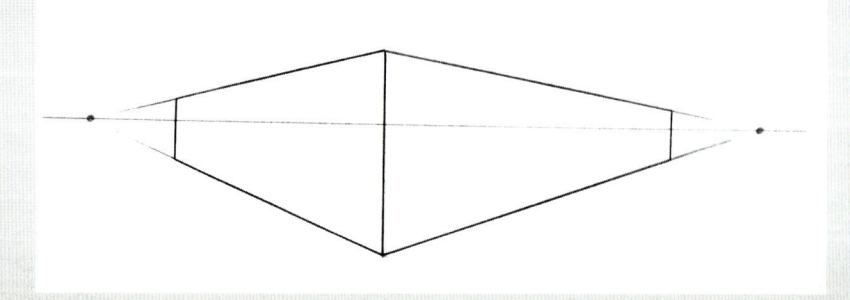

24

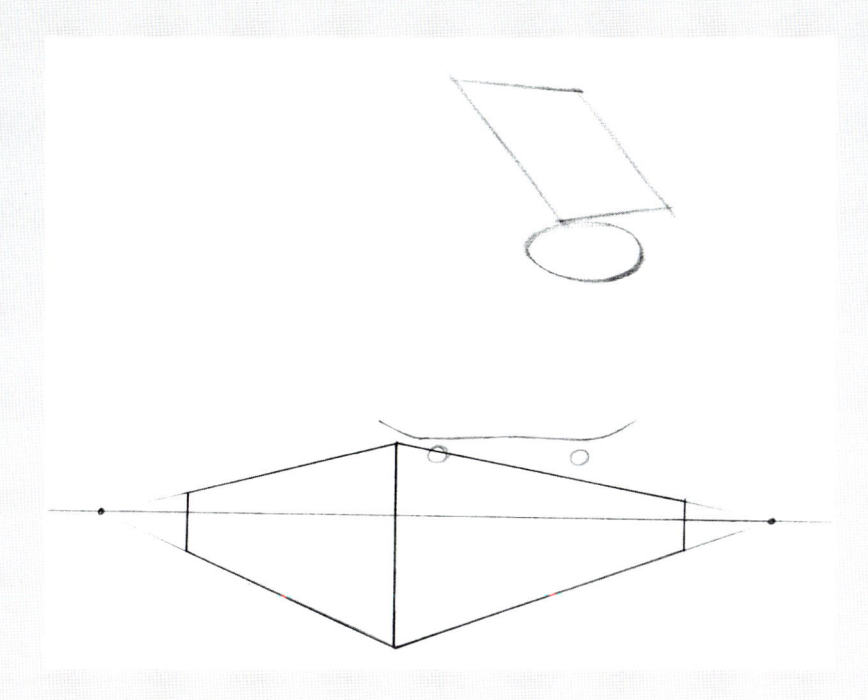

3 Sketch the shapes for his body. Carefully draw an angled line for the position of his skateboard. Notice that each end of the skateboard angles upward. Next, add two small circles for the wheels.

You can erase the perspective guidelines and the part of the horizon line that is behind the cube, where you can't see it.

Video game designers use perspective when designing video games. They can plan the way a certain environment will look with sketches, which are also called layouts. Video game designers make their final drawings on a computer.

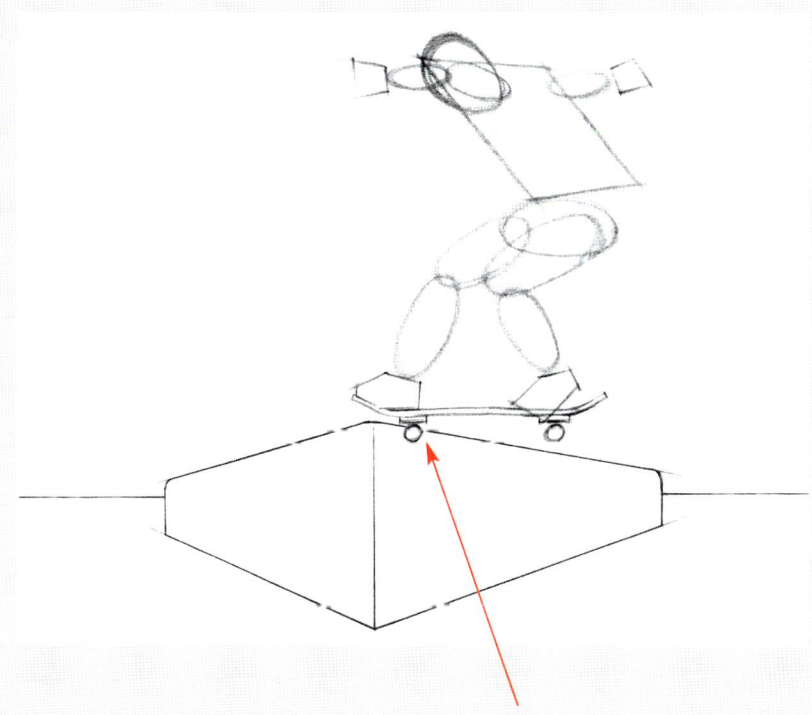

4 The skateboarder's upper body is twisting away from you. His center of gravity is balanced over the axle touching the cube. Sketch the four ovals that make his legs and the shapes for his shoes. Next, sketch the ovals for his arms and an egg shape for the position of his head. Add the shapes for his hands and the features of his skateboard.

The rear axle is balanced on the edge of the cube.

25

5 Check to see if the shapes you've drawn look balanced over the rear wheel. This is the point where the skateboarder pivots to turn his skateboard. Continue by drawing the outlines that form his body. Draw the contours of the folds in his clothing. Add details of his hair and face.

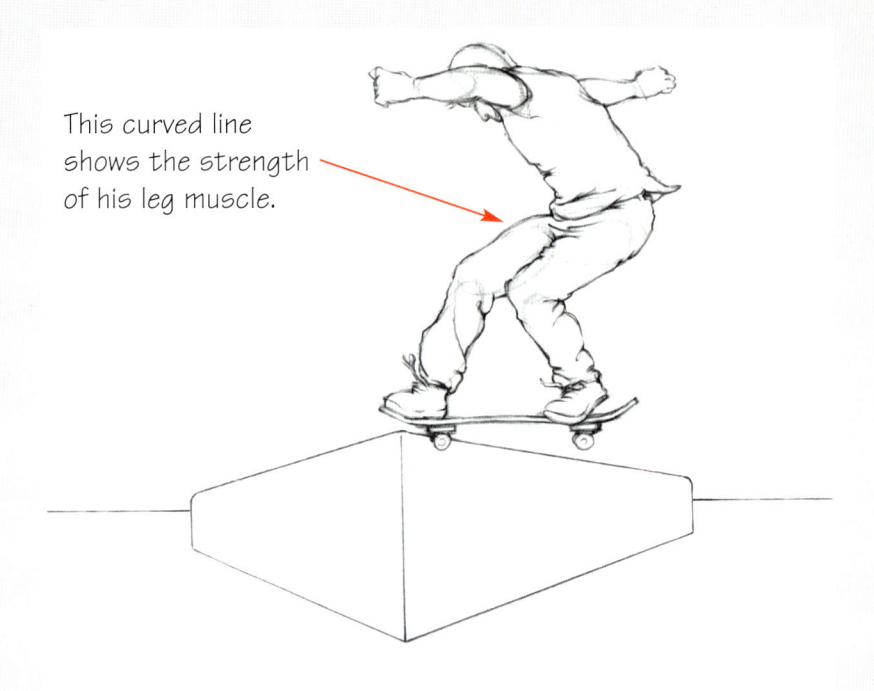

This curved line shows the strength of his leg muscle.

6 Finish your picture by carefully drawing darker contour lines. Add a gray tone for shadows on the wall of the cube facing away from the light source. Add shading to his body and clothing where less light shines. Notice the darkest shadows are areas in the folds of his clothing.

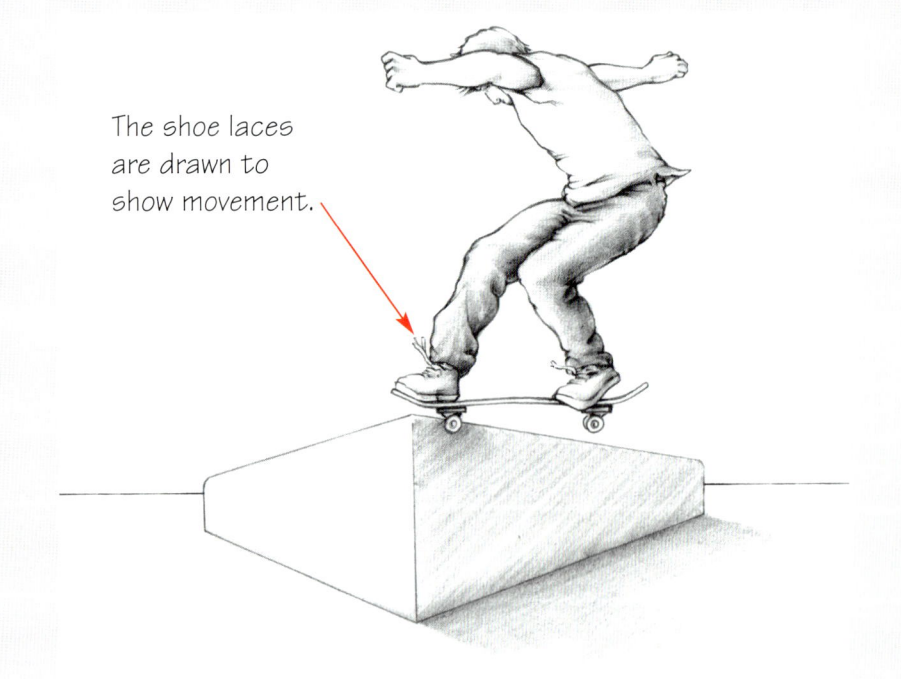

The shoe laces are drawn to show movement.

The skater's body and the cube cast a shadow on the ground.

Which Pencil Should You Use?

A standard "2B" or "2SOFT"' pencil works well for most drawings, but other pencils can make your drawing even more interesting.

Pencils are numbered according to how hard or soft the lead is. You'll find this number written on the pencil. A number combined with the letter "H" means the lead is hard (2H, 3H, 4H, etc.). When you draw with hard leads, the larger the number you use, the lighter and thinner your lines will be.

A number combined with the letter "B" means the lead is soft (2B, 4B, 6B, etc.). The lines you draw will get darker and thicker with larger numbers. Sometimes you will read "2SOFT" or "2B" on standard pencils used for schoolwork. When you see the letter "F" on a pencil, it means the pencil is of medium hardness.

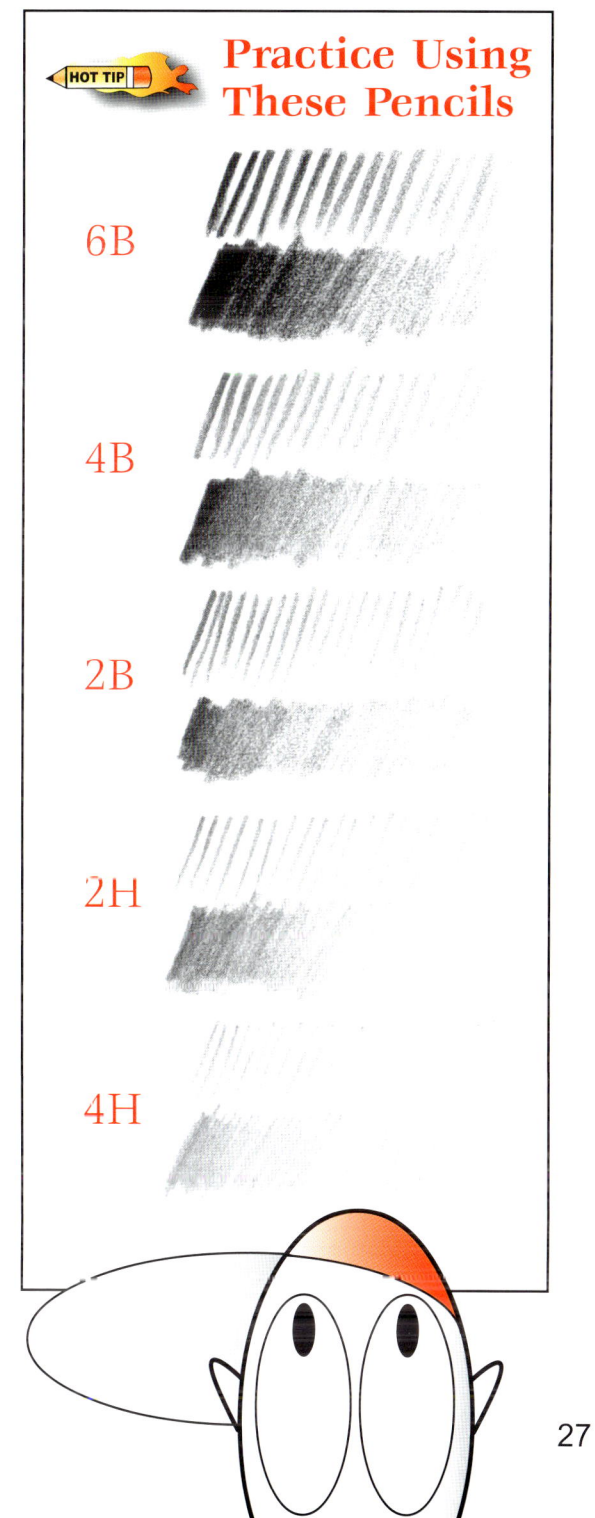

HOT TIP

Practice Using These Pencils

6B

4B

2B

2H

4H

Drawing with Color

By using colored pencils, you can make the picture of a surfer more exciting. Use cool colors (blue and green) for the wave and warm colors (yellow and red) for his body.

Surfer

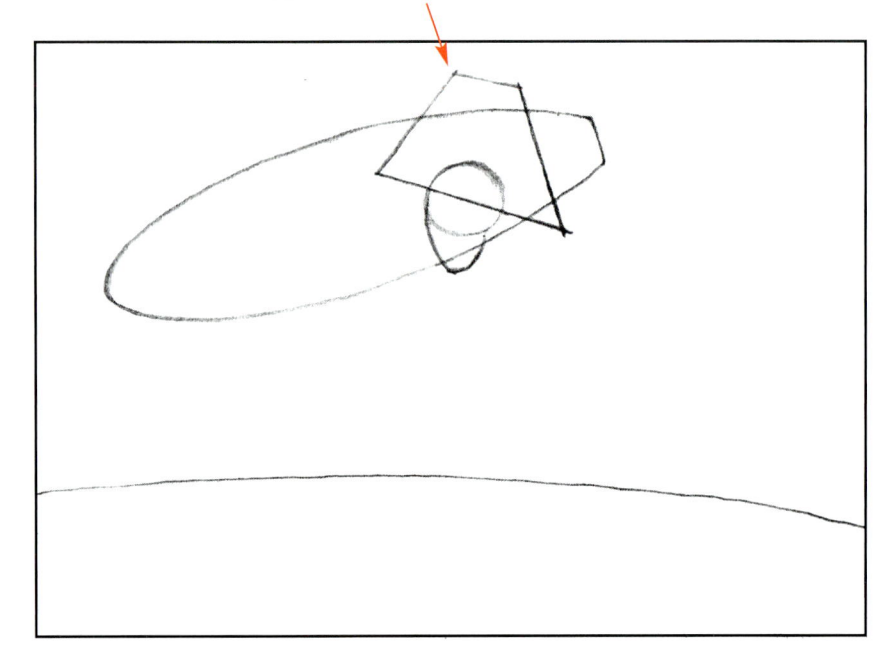

This shape will be his strong back and shoulder muscles.

1. Start your composition with a standard number 2 pencil. The surfer is performing an aerial high above the top of the wave. You don't have to draw the entire face of the wave. A curved line makes the top edge of the wave. Sketch the shape that shows the position of the surfboard. Next, draw the shapes for his body and head. Remember to draw light guidelines so they will be easy to erase before adding color.

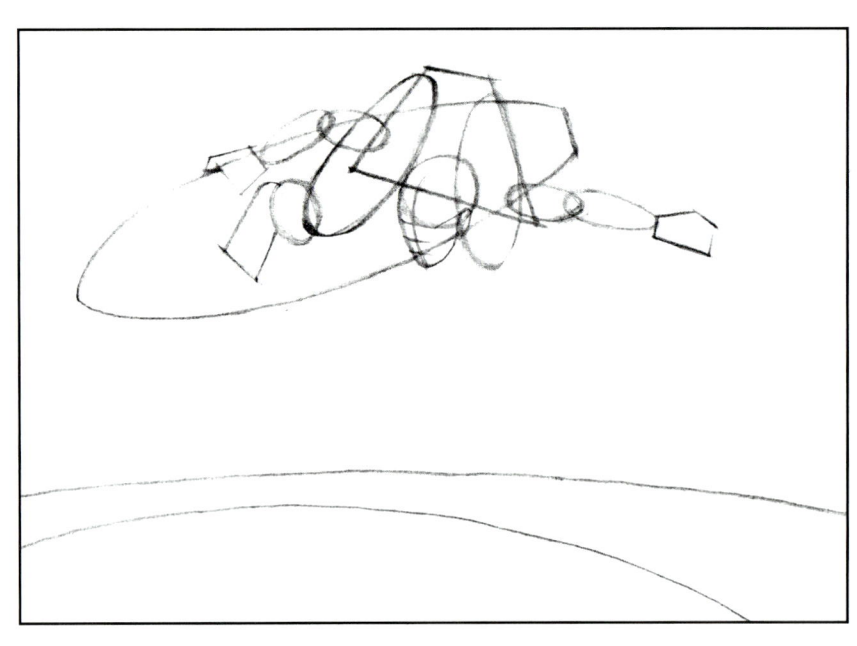

2. The surfer's body is crouched, with a low center of gravity. His feet are apart for stability. Draw large ovals for his strong legs. Next, make the ovals for both arms. Add the shapes for his hands and feet. Sketch guidelines for making a three-quarter view face. To learn more about drawing faces, see page 11. Draw another curved line that shows the breaking wave.

You can't see the entire length of the surfer's leg. So you must draw its foreshortened form.

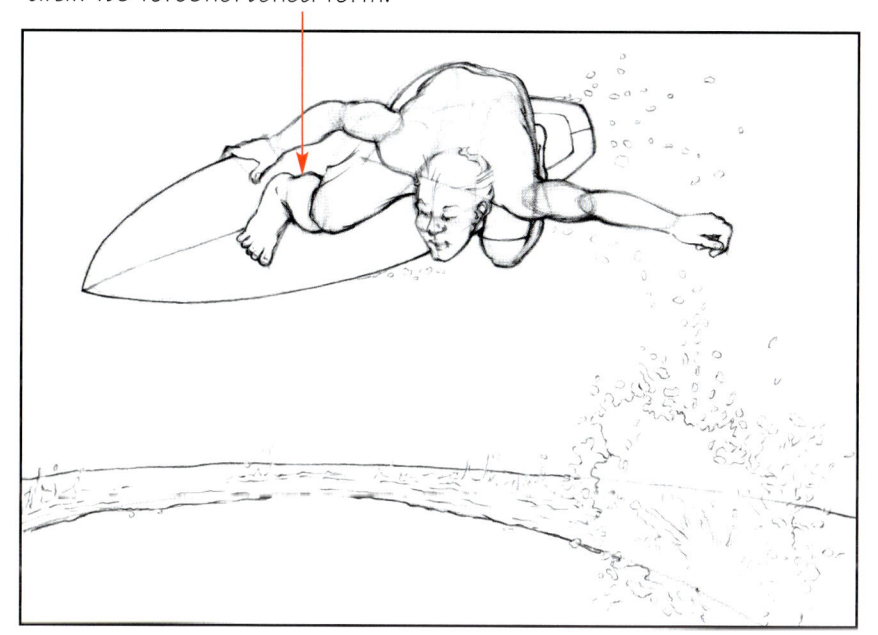

3 Take time to create the contour lines that form the muscular body of the surfer. Carefully draw the outlines of his foot and hands. Next, make the outline of the surfboard. Draw whitewater droplets that show the movement of the surfboard. When you like the lines you've drawn, carefully erase the guidelines and prepare to add color.

Primary Colors
red yellow blue

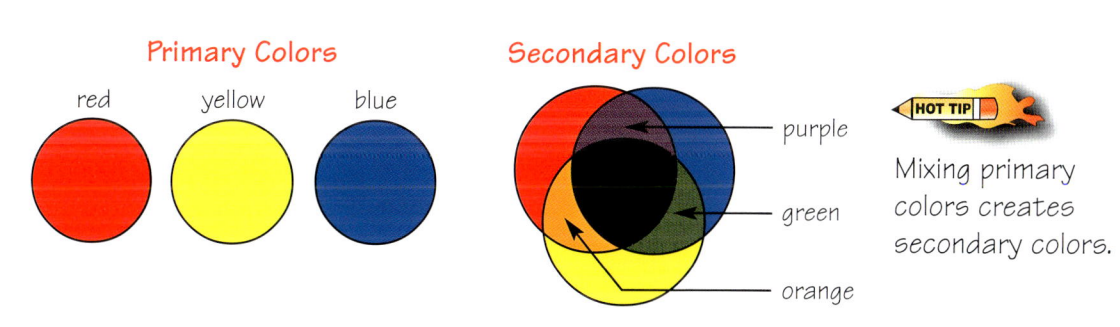

Secondary Colors
purple
green
orange

HOT TIP
Mixing primary colors creates secondary colors.

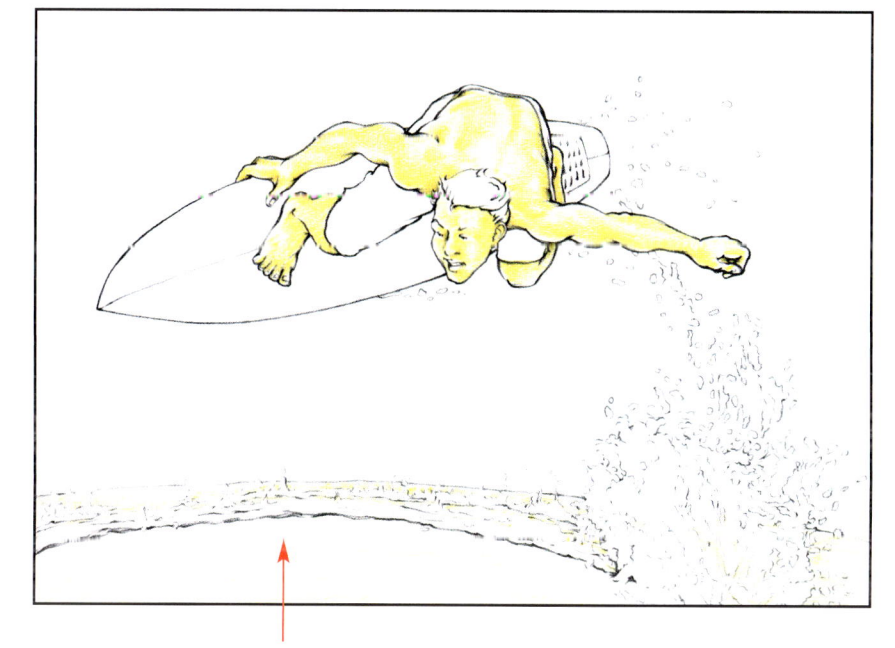

Adding one color on top of another while drawing is called layering. To learn how to layer primary colors, try using only yellow, blue, red, and black in this drawing.

4 Start by lightly shading the surfer's body with a yellow pencil. Think about the direction from where the light source is shining. Apply more pressure to darken areas where there are shadows.

Apply a light layer of yellow on this part of the wave to make green.

29

5 Before finishing his body, add a layer of blue to the wave. While holding your pencil on its side, apply blue to the wave. Breaking waves are often a greenish-blue color. What happens when blue and yellow are mixed? You can add blue to the background for the sky. Make it darker at the bottom and lighter as you move to the top of the picture.

Mixing Colored Pencils Is Fun!

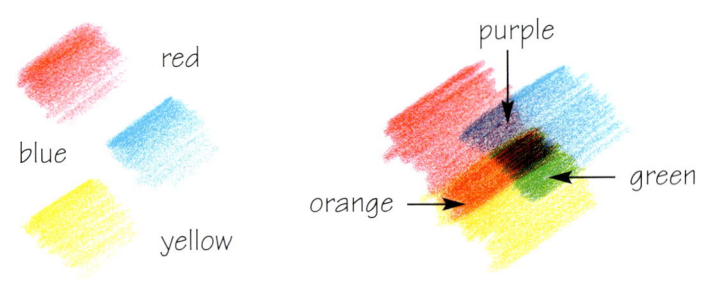

red
blue
yellow

purple
orange
green

Highlights and shadows make realistic details.

6 Fun things start to happen when you add red to the surfer's body. Mixing yellow and red creates a flesh tone. Mix different colors and make a pattern for his board shorts. You can add a color for the surfboard, too. Next, use your black pencil to lightly blend the areas of shadows. Remember to make darker shadows that are farther away from the light source. Shading with black creates the 3-D form of the surfer and the wave.

HOT TIP This basic pose can also be used when drawing skateboarders and snowboarders performing aerials.

30

The Artist's Studio

Artists need a special place where they can relax and concentrate on their work.

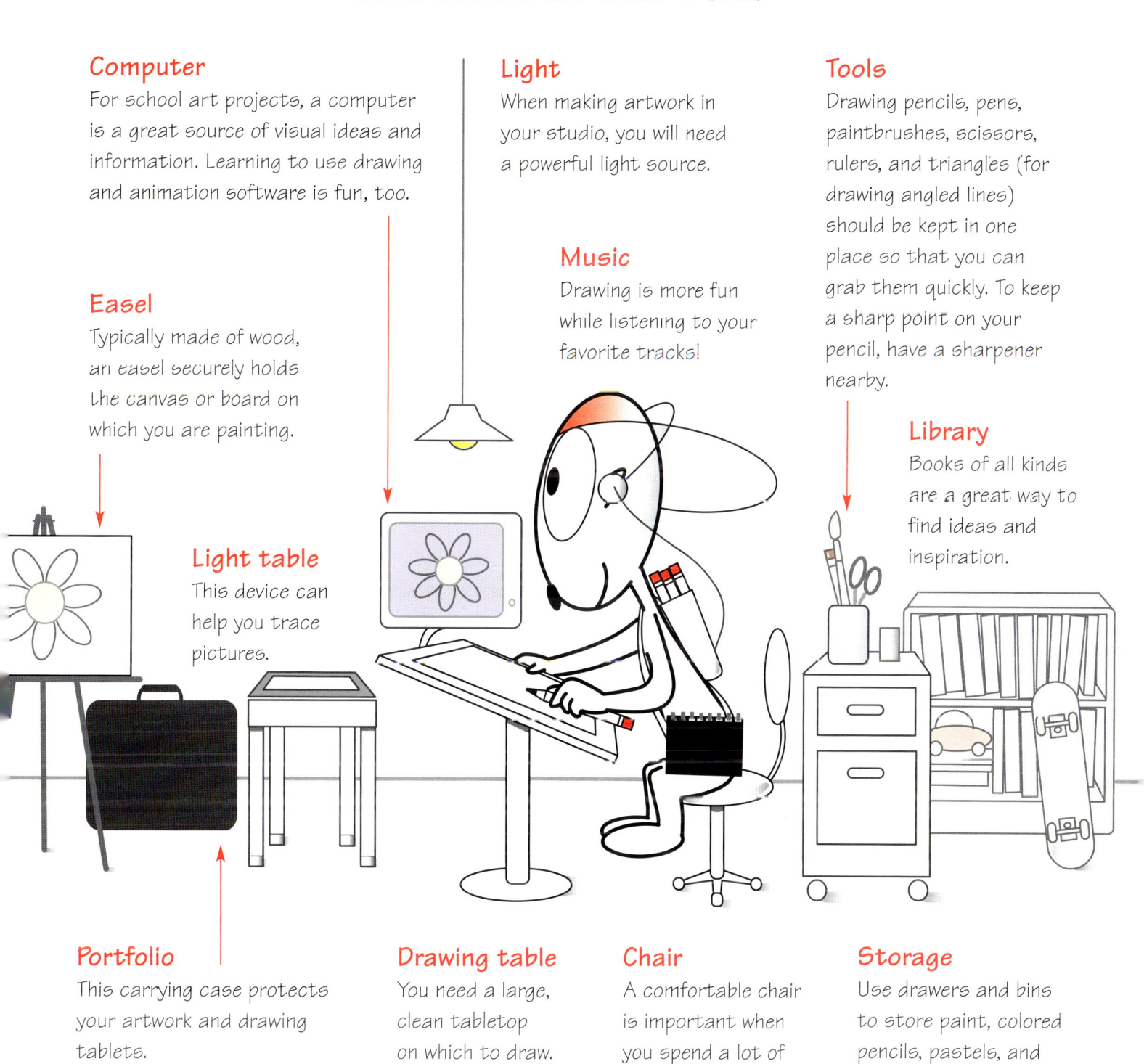

Computer
For school art projects, a computer is a great source of visual ideas and information. Learning to use drawing and animation software is fun, too.

Easel
Typically made of wood, an easel securely holds the canvas or board on which you are painting.

Light table
This device can help you trace pictures.

Light
When making artwork in your studio, you will need a powerful light source.

Music
Drawing is more fun while listening to your favorite tracks!

Tools
Drawing pencils, pens, paintbrushes, scissors, rulers, and triangles (for drawing angled lines) should be kept in one place so that you can grab them quickly. To keep a sharp point on your pencil, have a sharpener nearby.

Library
Books of all kinds are a great way to find ideas and inspiration.

Portfolio
This carrying case protects your artwork and drawing tablets.

Drawing table
You need a large, clean tabletop on which to draw.

Chair
A comfortable chair is important when you spend a lot of time drawing.

Storage
Use drawers and bins to store paint, colored pencils, pastels, and other supplies.

Glossary

A **cast shadow** is the shadow that a person, animal, or object throws on the ground, a wall, or other feature.

A **contour** is the outline of something; in your drawings, a contour line follows the natural shape of the sports action figures.

A **form shadow** is a shadow in a drawing that shows the form or shape of a person, animal, or object.

A **highlight** is the area or areas in a drawing that receive the most light from the light source.

A **horizontal** line moves from side to side; a person lying down is in a horizontal position.

An **outline** is a line that shows the shape of an object, animal, or person.

Perspective is the art of picturing objects on a flat surface, like a piece of paper, so that they appear to be in the distance.

Proportions are the relations between two or more things in terms of their size; if something is in proportion, all its parts are in proper relation to each other.

A **vertical** line is drawn straight up and down; a person standing up is in a vertical position.

Index

background, 22, 23, 30
color, 18, 28–30
composition, 24, 28
contour, 9, 10, 11, 14, 15, 17, 19, 21, 23, 26, 29
foreground, 22
guideline, 10–11, 14, 16, 17, 18, 19, 20, 24, 25, 28, 29
highlight, 19, 30
horizon line, 24–25
light, 18–19
light source, 19, 26, 29, 30
line, 9, 10
outline, 9, 10, 11, 14–15, 17, 19, 21, 23, 26, 29
pattern, 20–21, 22, 30
pencils, selecting, 27
perspective, 24–25
shadow, 18–19, 26, 29, 30
shape, 7, 8, 9
space, 24
studio, artist's, 31
texture, 22–23
three-dimensional (3D) form, 16–17, 30

About the Author

Rob Court is a designer and illustrator. He started the Scribbles Institute™ to help people learn about the importance of drawing and visual art.